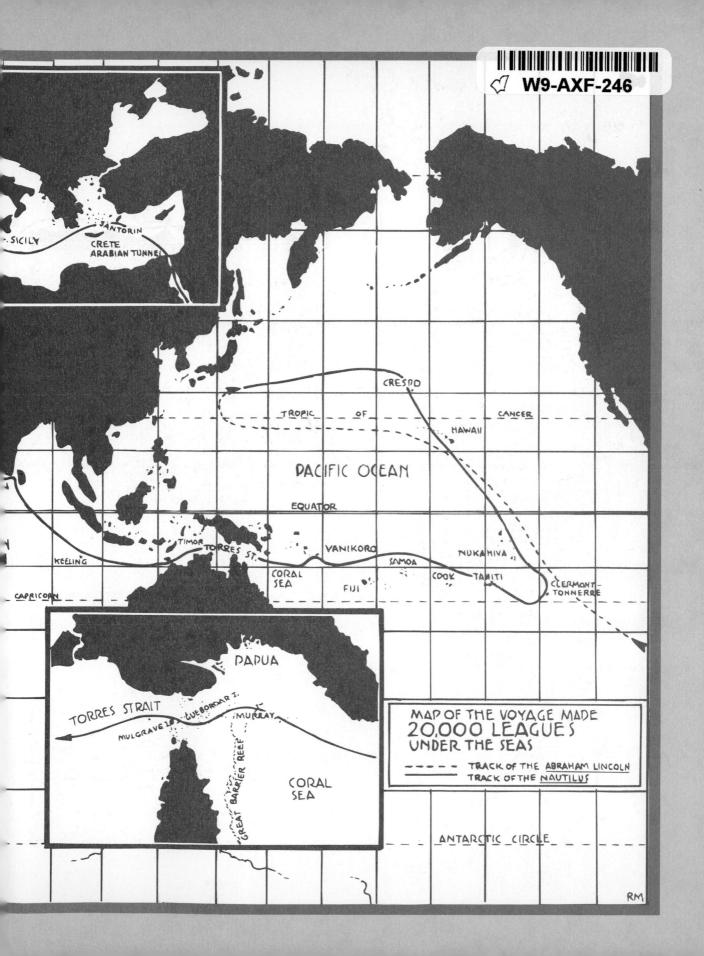

MAP OF THE VOYAGE MADE
20,000 LEAGUES
UNDER THE SEAS

------- TRACK OF THE ABRAHAM LINCOLN
——— TRACK OF THE NAUTILUS

TWENTY THOUSAND LEAGUES UNDER THE SEAS

Illustrated by
RON MILLER

Adapted from the novel by
Jules Verne

The Unicorn Publishing House
New Jersey

TWENTY THOUSAND LEAGUES

The year 1866 brought with it a big mystery. Sailors on ships all over the world had reported seeing a strange object in the oceans. A huge, glowing *thing*. Was it an unknown sea monster? No one knew. One ship had met the strange creature and reported that it sent two sprays of water 150 feet into the air! No whale could do that. Three days after one ship reported sighting the monster, another ship 2,000 miles away saw it! What sea monster could swim that fast? Finally, the captain of a ship was able to measure the size of the monster. He thought it was more than 300 feet long! No known sea creature grew so large. What was it? The whole world wanted to know. Scientists argued between themselves as to what the creature might be. Could it be a whale? A giant squid? No one could say for sure.

Soon it became quite important to find out what the creature was. A ship called the *Scotia* was attacked by the monster! A big hole was punched in its side. It was just barely able to get safely back to port. When the *Scotia* was put into dry dock for repair, everyone was surprised by the shape of the hole. It was a perfect triangle! What kind of monster could punch a hole like that?

The public called for the government to do something about this dangerous creature. And that's where I came in. My name is Professor Aronnax. I am a scientist at the Museum of Natural History in Paris, France. I was collecting samples in the American West when I first heard about the strange sea monster. The

Americans were sending a ship to find out what it was. Think of my surprise when I was asked to join the journey! It seems that a scientist was badly needed. The Navy was aware that I had written a book about the ocean and its creatures.

Of course I accepted the offer. Taking my assistant, Conseil, with me, I went to New York where I boarded the ship. I met the captain, Commander Farragut. He introduced me to the master harpooner on board. His name was Ned Land.

Soon smoke was pouring out of the smokestacks. We were on our way. Hundreds of people lined the shore, waving us farewell.

Since the monster had been last seen in the Pacific Ocean, we had a long journey ahead of us. I had plenty of time to get to know Ned Land. As a scientist, I was interested in what he knew about whales. I asked him what he thought of the monster.

"Monster! That's silly!" he said.

"Don't you think there is a monster, Ned?"

"Of course not; there are no such things!"

"Well, then, what happened to the *Scotia?*"

Ned didn't have an answer to that. We sailed past the Straits of Magellan and into the Pacific Ocean. All eyes were glued to the sea, looking for any sign of the monster. The captain offered a reward to the first man who sighted the creature. But day after day passed without a single clue. We sailed back and forth for weeks. Finally, Commander Farragut told us that if the monster wasn't found soon, he'd have to give up the search.

"This is my last chance to win that reward," said Ned, determined to spot the creature.

"I'll just be glad to get back to Paris," said Conseil.

But events unfolded that night to make a return to Paris impossible. In fact, we would soon be fighting for our lives! Late that night a cry arose from up on deck. I could hear Ned shouting, "There it is! The thing itself!"

Everyone rushed to the railing. There, not more than 200

yards off the port side, was a bright, glowing patch beneath the waves. The captain ordered the ship closer, but the strange glow kept moving away. Soon he gave the order to his gunners to hit it. The cannons fired, but the shells seemed just to bounce off.

"Look out!" a sailor cried.

The monster was rushing the ship! There was a very loud crash and I found myself thrown clear over the railing. The last thing I remember was hitting the water.

When I came to, Conseil was swimming beside me, holding my head above the waves.

"What are you doing here?" I asked.

"I'm your assistant; wherever you go, I go too," he replied rather matter-of-factly.

Conseil was truly amazing! I looked around for the *ship*, but it was nowhere to be seen. I thought that the monster must have sunk it, but Conseil said that the ship had steamed away.

What were we to do? We were drifting in the middle of the Pacific Ocean! We swam for a long time, but it was getting harder to keep afloat. Just when I thought that we were lost, I saw something floating in the water near us.

"Help! Help!" we cried.

I thought I heard a voice call out. It sounded like Ned! As I swam closer to the dark object, I saw that it was not like any boat I had ever seen. It was just a long, black hump, like half a cigar, and the top was only a few feet above the water. Someone helped us to climb onto the thing. I saw that it was Ned.

"Ned!" I said. "Were you thrown into the sea as well?"

"Yes, but luckily I found safety on this floating island."

"Island?"

"Yes," he said. "An island made of iron!"

Sure enough, when I looked closely, I saw that the thing I was standing on was made of iron plates welded together. I had heard of the iron ships the Americans had built during the Civil

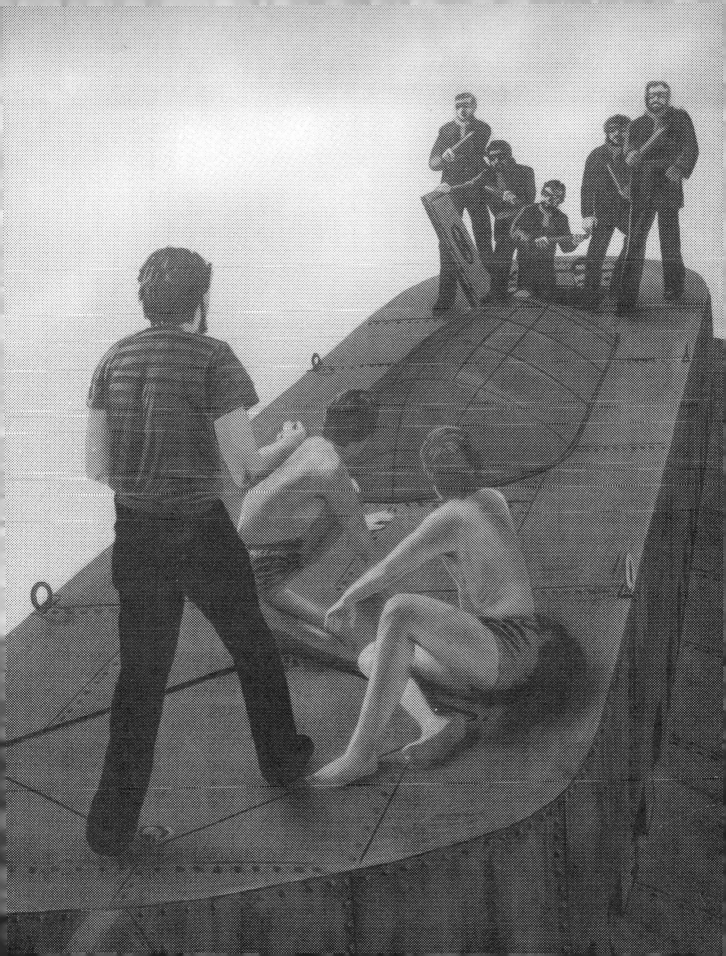

War, but they were nothing like this! I couldn't think what it could be. We started pounding on the thing. There was a clanking sound, and a hatch opened. We were surprised when eight masked men came out of it. They carried clubs, so we didn't argue with them. They forced us through the hatch and down a ladder. We were shut up in a little iron room. We were prisoners! Ned became furious.

"Confound it! This is poor treatment for castaways!"

"Calm yourself, Ned," I said. "No one has hurt us."

"Not yet!" he answered. It was quite some time before we heard the bolt of our door rattling. Two men came in. One was a short strong-looking sailor, but the other was very tall. He had a cold, intelligent look. He was the one in charge. Neither one said a word to us. We tried to speak to the tall man but he acted as though he didn't hear us. After a few moments, he and his companion left.

"Well!" Ned said. "We spoke to those men in French, English, German, and Latin! Are they deaf? If I get my hands on . . ."

"Being angry is not going to get us anywhere," I said.

Soon the short man returned with a tray of food. There was fish, of course, but many other things I did not know. Everything was delicious. We slept well after our meal. However, we did not see the sailor until the next day. Ned had had enough. As soon as the sailor entered, Ned grabbed the man and began choking him! I was rushing to the sailor's rescue when I heard a voice.

"Please, quiet yourself, Mr. Land. And you, Professor Aronnax, please be good enough to listen to me."

It was the mysterious tall commander who had spoken. Ned was so surprised that he let the sailor go. After a few moments of silence, the commander spoke again.

"Gentlemen, I could have talked to you when you first spoke, but I wanted first to study you and to find out who you were. I am very annoyed that you have come here. I am a man who has

broken all ties with the human race, and now here you are to trouble me."

"It was by accident that we came to be here," I said.

"An accident?" he replied. "Was it an accident that your ship chased and shot at me?"

"A ship! We thought it . . . you were a sea monster!"

"Tell me the truth, Professor. Wouldn't your captain just as soon have chased and shot at a submarine as a sea monster?"

I had no answer. The captain would have thought it was his duty to destroy such a submarine, if he had known it existed.

"I have the right," he went on, "to treat you as prisoners of war. You are free to roam about the ship, but you can never leave it."

With these words, the commander led me from the cell into a big room. I gasped with surprise. It was like a museum!

"I see you like my collections, Professor," he said, smiling. "Let me welcome you aboard the *Nautilus*. You may call me Captain Nemo."

I thought that the name suited this strange man, because *nemo* was the Latin word for "no one". He continued to speak.

"For many years I have collected the riches of the seas. Here you will find samples that museums would pay fortunes for. I think that as a scientist you may enjoy your stay with me, sir."

I knew that he was right. A trip in the *Nautilus* would be a golden chance for me. I looked about me. There were beautiful seashells in glass cases. There were stuffed fish and other sea animals. And at one end of the room there was a large organ. But best of all, there were two big windows. I could see hundreds of fish swimming past the *Nautilus!*

"I have a thousand questions, Captain."

"Please have a seat, and I will try to answer them."

"First, I would like to know where you came from, and why you built this submarine."

"Who I am is of no concern to you. You only need to know that I am someone who has decided to be done with the human race, for reasons that I will not tell. I no longer have any contact with land. I get everything I need from the sea."

"You must love the sea," I said.

"Yes, I love it!" he replied. "The sea is everything! The air is pure and healthy, and a man need never be lonely here. Life is stirring all around him. The sea belongs to no one. Men can fight their wars on its waves, but thirty feet down, all is peace!"

"That is why you built the *Nautilus?*"

"Yes. I found men for my crew who thought as I do."

"What powers the *Nautilus?* I don't see a steam engine."

"For an answer to that you must come with me, if you please."

Captain Nemo led me down a long hall into another room. It was the engine room of the submarine. Huge machines were humming. "Everything on the ship is run by electricity, Professor," Nemo said.

"Electricity!" I cried.

"Yes, from powerful batteries that I made myself. Electricity runs these motors. It gives us light, and we even cook with it."

"How do you gather your samples or get your food?"

"I was just about to invite all of you to join me on a trip."

"A trip?"

"Yes. A trip to the bottom of the sea."

Captain Nemo led me to a small room, where I met Conseil and Ned. Here Nemo showed us how to get into some heavy rubber diving suits. Then he showed us some round metal tanks.

"These contain air. You wear them on your backs, with hoses to carry the air to your helmets. The air is under pressure, so there is enough in each tank to last for several hours."

"Will we have any weapons?" asked Ned.

"Yes," replied the Captain. "These guns fire special bullets. The bullets are like little batteries. They will shock anything

they touch."

The helmets were placed on our heads. The room was sealed and began to fill with water. As soon as it was full, another door opened. We stepped out onto the floor of the ocean.

It was a wonderful experience to walk underwater. The plants and coral were like a garden of flowers. Hundreds of colorful fish swam over our heads like butterflies. It was an amazing experience. All my life I had studied the creatures that live in the sea, but never before had I been able to see them alive in their own world! Truly, Nemo's ship was wonderful!

We had walked some miles, far from the submarine. As I walked around a large coral, I came face to face with a giant sea spider! It had enormous claws. Just as the creature was about to attack, Nemo ran forward and hit the monster with the butt of his gun. It was decided we should return to the ship at once.

I spent the next few days studying sea life and reading from Nemo's library. Conseil took notes. Ned, however, was not very happy. Being a harpooner, he didn't like being shut up inside.

One day, as I was reading, there was a crash, and the submarine shook fearfully. Captain Nemo came into the study.

"An accident, Captain?" I asked.

"In a way, Professor," he answered. "We were going through a reef and ran aground. We'll have to wait for the tide to free us."

I went on deck. The jagged reef was all around us. Nearby was a small island. The Captain had followed me on deck. I asked Nemo if we might be able to go ashore. After all, there was no way to escape.

"Of course," he said. "I'll get a boat ready."

The little boat took us to the island quickly. We hiked far into the jungle. We were able to find birds, which we shot for dinner. We also found some fruits and vegetables to take back to the *Nautilus*. We were heading back to the ship, when suddenly a stone fell at our feet!

"What was that?" cried Ned.

Just then a second stone knocked a bird from Conseil's hands. "Savages!" he cried.

Sure enough, twenty natives ran out of the jungle, waving spears and knives. They hardly looked friendly.

"Run for the boat!" shouted Ned.

We ran as fast as we could. Stones and arrows fell all around us. We threw everything we had into the boat and jumped in. We pulled away from the shore just as the natives reached the water. Luckily, they didn't want to swim after us.

"That was a close call!" said Ned.

When we got back to the *Nautilus*, I ran to the Captain.

"Well, Professor, did you have a good hunt?"

"Yes, but we brought some bipeds back with us," I replied.

"What bipeds?"

"Savages!"

"How many, Professor?"

"At least a hundred."

Up on deck Nemo's men shouted that natives were coming in their own boats. Spears and arrows began to fly, and the men ran below. I soon heard the natives running about on deck.

"You had better close the hatch," I said.

"Why, Professor?" Nemo asked.

"Why! So they won't come down here and kill us!" I cried.

"There is nothing to worry about," he said.

"But the hatch is open!"

"Yes, but they won't come in," he said.

I soon found out the reason why. As the natives tried to come down the ladder, they jumped back in pain.

"The ladder is electrified," said Captain Nemo. "It will give a powerful shock to anyone that touches it."

"Well, it certainly works!" said Ned, who had the misfortune of touching it.

The Captain turned off the electricity and we went on deck. The natives had fled in terror in their boats. Before long the tide came in and the *Nautilus* was free again.

We cruised for many days without anything exciting happening. Even though I knew that I was a prisoner, I was happy. I was seeing so many wonderful things. I didn't really care if I ever got back home. As for Conseil, he was a loyal assistant. As long as he was with me, he was happy too. It was Ned who worried me. Escape was all he could think of.

One morning, Captain Nemo came to me very upset.

"Professor," he asked me, "you are a doctor as well, aren't you?"

"Yes, I am," I said. "Is something wrong?"

"I'm afraid so. Can you come with me?"

"Of course," I said, and followed the Captain. He took me to a part of the submarine I hadn't seen before. It was the crew's quarters. A man was lying in one of the bunks. He had a very bad injury to his head. I examined him, then took Captain Nemo to one side, where the injured sailor couldn't hear me.

"Will he live?" asked Nemo.

"No, I am afraid not. He will be dead in just a few hours. There's nothing to be done."

I saw tears form in the eyes of a man I had thought incapable of compassion for other human beings. "Thank you, Professor," he said. "You may return to your room."

A few hours later, the Captain came to my room. He asked us to join him in another underwater trip. Soon we were walking on the ocean bottom again. We came to a large open area, and I was suddenly aware that there were crosses made from coral everywhere. It was an underwater cemetery! I had seen that some of the men were carrying a large object. I now knew that it was a coffin. It was put down into a hole, which was then filled in with coral. We bowed our heads for a few moments and then

returned to the ship.

A few days later Captain Nemo invited us once again to venture out into the sea. We were near Ceylon, where there are large pearl fisheries. The Captain thought that it might be interesting to see how pearls were gathered. We put on our suits and left the submarine.

When we reached the pearl fishery, we watched the divers work. They would tie heavy stones to their feet, jump into the water, and gather as many oysters as they could. When a diver ran out of breath, he untied the stones and swam to the surface.

We were about to leave when a dark shadow passed overhead. It was a huge shark! It headed straight for one of the divers. As it circled the poor man, it struck him with its tail. The diver was knocked out and sank to the bottom. The shark turned to attack. Just then, Captain Nemo leaped in front of the shark. He had his knife in his hand and grabbed on to one of the shark's fins. It was the most thrilling battle I had ever seen. Nemo braced himself and waited for the shark to attack. When it rushed at him, he quickly threw himself to one side. Then he stabbed the shark with the dagger. Blood poured out of the side of the shark. It was so thick, I could hardly see the Captain. A terrible fight followed. The shark opened its mouth to bite him. Nemo held tight to the fin as the shark rolled over and over. Just when I thought the Captain was lost, I saw his knife plunge again into the side of the shark. The shark sank to the bottom. Captain Nemo brought the diver to the surface and placed him in his boat. The diver would be amazed when he awoke to find himself safe and sound in his own boat!

I just couldn't understand Nemo. Why did he care so much about his crewmen and a pearl diver when he would attack and sink ships full of men without a second thought?

We continued our trip. We entered the Red Sea. The *Nautilus* passed through a secret underwater tunnel that connected the

Red Sea with the Mediterranean. We soon found ourselves off the island of Crete. It belonged to Greece, Nemo said. But Greece had been defeated by its enemy, Turkey. Many Greeks were trying to revolt against the Turks and win their country back. But the Greeks were very poor, and couldn't buy weapons or help. As the Captain was telling us all this, Conseil suddenly cried out in surprise. We went to the window to see what it was. There was someone swimming outside! When Captain Nemo saw him, he gave a signal, which the swimmer answered.

Then the swimmer rose to the surface of the water.

"Don't be alarmed," said Captain Nemo. "This man is a bold diver. He is more at home in the water than on land."

"Do you know this man, Captain?"

"I do," said Captain Nemo. He turned and rang a bell. Several strong crewmen came in and carried out a large iron chest, which I had seen sitting on the floor.

"What was that?" I asked.

"Gold," replied Nemo, "to help the Greeks."

"Gold!" I said. "Why, there must have been hundreds of pounds in that chest! Where could you get so much gold?"

"If you really want to know, I will be happy to show you."

I had to wait several days, until we left the Mediterranean and were sailing up the coast of Spain. The *Nautilus* stopped and Captain Nemo asked me to get into my diving suit once again. The Captain, several of his men, and I left the submarine. We walked a mile or two; then I saw them rising from the sea floor—sunken ships, more than half a dozen of them! They looked very old, as though they had been there for hundreds of years. Then I saw what Captain Nemo's men were doing. They were carrying a chest from the ship. I knew then what these ships were. They were Spanish treasure ships! Each one had millions of dollars in gold, silver, and jewels. We were visiting Captain Nemo's private bank!

When we returned to the ship, Captain Nemo looked at me. "Did you know that the sea had such riches?" he asked.

"I knew there were many shipwrecks in this region," I said.

"There are wrecks here, and in the oceans around the world," said Nemo. "I have become a very rich man, Professor Aronnax."

A few days later I was invited on another underwater trip. What amazing thing was the Captain going to show me now? He and I went alone this time. It was a very long walk over rough ground. I was getting very tired. However, I grew curious as we approached a strange glow that was just up ahead. It grew brighter as we came closer. As we came around a bend, I could finally see the source of the eerie light. It was the eruption of an underwater volcano! And at the base of the mountain, lit by the flickering glow, was an ancient city! It was in ruins, destroyed when it sank beneath the sea. How many thousands of years ago, I could not guess.

I could see fallen buildings, temples, and beautiful statues stretching out across the sea floor. It was amazing! But what city could this be, lost beneath the waves for all these centuries? Captain Nemo could see that I was confused. He took a piece of chalk out and on some black rock wrote one word: ATLANTIS.

It was the legendary city that the world thought was only a myth, a fable. Yet it was before me! Ah! Why did I have such little time? I would have liked to walk through this lost city. What history was lying there! I would have liked to see the buildings of its people. I would have liked to study the great city and see how its people had lived. But I knew that we had to return to the ship. The walk had been long. We would run out of air soon. All the way back to the ship I thought about what I had seen. The ruined buildings, the fallen temples, the broken arches with their great pillars lying on the sea floor. It was quite a sight! I also thought of Captain Nemo. Would he have liked that ancient world better than this modern one?

Back at the *Nautilus*, the Captain told me that the ship's batteries were getting low, and that we would have to stop at his base to recharge them. So Captain Nemo had a base! This would be interesting news for Ned! Where could the base be? Some secret island perhaps? We would soon find out.

After a day or so had gone by, Captain Nemo told me that we had come to his base. I went up on deck. But what was this? It was the middle of the day, yet it was black as night! I looked straight up. There was a bright blue circle over my head, like a huge moon. I knew then what it was—a circle of daylight. His secret base was inside an extinct volcano. An underwater tunnel led into it. The volcano was hollow. The circle of light at the top was the volcano's crater.

Captain Nemo let Ned, Conseil, and me go ashore while his men worked on the batteries. This almost drove Ned mad. There could be no escape from this island, since the walls of the cavern curved overhead, making climbing impossible. We gathered eggs from seabirds' nests and then returned to the submarine.

The next day the *Nautilus* was in a strange part of the Atlantic Ocean. It was an area called the Sargasso Sea, a kind of sea-within-a-sea in the middle of the Atlantic. It was large, and shaped like a circle, and seaweed grew very thickly there. Legends told of ships that had been trapped in it, unable to escape. However, in real life, the weed did not grow thickly enough to be any real danger.

We wandered around the Atlantic for several days. Captain Nemo came to my cabin one day and asked if I would like to see how deep the *Nautilus* could go.

"Yes, I would, very much," I replied.

The Captain gave the order. A few minutes later I could feel the submarine sinking.

"We are near a spot," said the Captain, "where scientists could not find the bottom even with a line 42,000 feet long."

"How deep are we now?" I asked.

The Captain looked at an instrument on the wall. "We are that deep now!"

I looked out the window. It was very dark. All I could see were a few black peaks rising from below. The *Nautilus* still sank, and I could hear its iron plates groaning under the huge pressure of the water.

"We are at a depth now of about 48,000 feet. That's about nine miles deep."

"Look at those strange rocks out there!" I said. "There is not a single living thing at this depth."

"We had better go up to the surface now before the *Nautilus* is crushed under this pressure," said Captain Nemo.

He gave a signal. "Hold on!" he cried. I barely had time to do so, when the *Nautilus* shot up like a balloon. We were going through the water so fast, the submarine was shaking! In just four minutes we went up the nine miles to the surface! The *Nautilus* shot out of the water like a flying fish. Then it fell back onto the waves with a huge splash.

A few days later, Ned, Conseil, and I were sitting on deck. Ned was telling us how bored he was. I could understand how he felt. He was a man of action, not a man of books like myself. Think of his great joy when he suddenly spotted a group of whales! He ran to the Captain to ask if he could hunt them. But Nemo said "no."

"There goes a whole fortune for a whaling ship!" Ned cried.

"The *Nautilus* is not a whaling ship," Captain Nemo said.

"Can't I chase them, just to remind myself of the hunt?"

"What for?" asked the Captain. "Just to kill them? That would be killing just for the sake of killing. I don't approve of killing for sport. Whalers are killing off whole species of the animal!"

There was nothing that Ned could say to make the Captain agree. He had to watch the group of whales swim peacefully

away. From that day on I noticed that Ned's hatred of Nemo grew greater. I promised myself to watch him closely.

Day after day the *Nautilus* went farther and farther south. Was Captain Nemo going to take us to the South Pole? I couldn't believe that even he would go that far. But before long we began to see icebergs forming in the frigid ocean. By week's end we were slipping through huge sheets of ice that covered the water.

The ice became so thick that I was afraid the *Nautilus* would become trapped.

"Don't worry, Professor," Nemo said. "The *Nautilus* will go farther south still!"

"Farther south! To the South Pole?"

"Of course."

I thought the Captain had gone mad. But still, hadn't the *Nautilus* already done amazing things?

"But," I asked, "how can the ship get over hundreds of miles of ice?"

"Not over, Professor, but under."

Now I understood what he was going to do. Beneath the ice was open water. We would sail beneath the ice cap to reach the South Pole. It was a wonderful idea.

The *Nautilus* dived. Very slowly it slipped beneath the ice. We had to go very carefully. If we crashed into the bottom of an iceberg, we could wreck the submarine.

Every once in a while there would be a bump when we would strike the bottom of the ice. We kept having to go deeper and deeper, as the ice above us got thicker and thicker. There was no sign of the ice's thinning as we neared the Pole. Already the air inside the ship was getting bad. What if we couldn't get to the top of the water at the South Pole? How could we get fresh air? If we took too long to reach the Pole, we would run out of air!

We tried several times to rise to the surface, but the ice was quite thick. Finally, we broke through. We rushed onto the deck.

The *Nautilus* floated in the middle of a huge sheet of ice.

"Are we at the Pole?" I asked.

"Not yet," Nemo said.

Again the *Nautilus* went under the water. The next time it came to the surface, there was open water around us, like a big lake surrounded by icebergs. Not far from us was a group of rocks. Captain Nemo took the small boat and rowed to the rocks. He climbed onto them and took some measurements.

"Is this the Pole?" I shouted.

"I will know in a moment," he replied.

Soon Captain Nemo looked up and called out proudly, "The South Pole!"

With these words he took out a large black flag. As it waved in the cold wind, I saw that it had his initial, "N," on it. I asked, "In whose name are you claiming the South Pole?"

"In my own!" he simply said, and then he returned to the submarine.

The *Nautilus* soon sank beneath the waves, and we were under way. In a day or two we would be free of the ice. It would be none too soon, as far as I was concerned!

I was quietly sleeping in my room the next morning, when I was awakened by a loud crash. I was thrown from my bed to the floor. I ran looking for Nemo. I found him in the museum.

"What happened?" I asked.

"An accident, I'm afraid," he replied.

"A serious one?"

"Perhaps," he said, looking a little worried. "As we were passing beneath an iceberg it turned over, trapping us under it."

"Can we get out?"

"We shall see!"

He went to his instruments and ordered the *Nautilus* to move ahead slowly. But the ship was blocked in the front. Nemo put the submarine in reverse. Once again we only moved a short dis-

tance before running into the ice.

"What does this mean?" I wanted to know.

"It means we're trapped. We cannot escape by going up or down, forward or backward!"

I went to tell Conseil and Ned the bad news. They wanted to know what would happen next.

"What does the Captain plan to do?" Ned asked.

"I don't know," I said.

"Well," Ned cried, "let's ask him!"

We returned to the museum, where the Captain was busy making plans. We asked him if there was any hope at all of escaping this prison of ice that surrounded us.

"There is one chance," he said. "The iceberg is too thick above us and in front and back. But it may be very thin beneath us. If we can make it a little thinner, the *Nautilus* may be able to break through."

"How can we do that?" we asked.

"We will have to go outside in our suits and dig a hole beneath the submarine! All of us will have to take turns working."

It was very hard work, trying to dig through the ice with picks and shovels. The water was freezing even in our suits. Even with all of his crew and our help, at the end of the first day the hole was not deep enough. And we only had a day of air left!

We worked all through the night, taking turns going out. The air inside the *Nautilus* was getting very hard to breathe. We were getting so tired we could hardly move. But still we kept working.

Our time was almost up. I was in the museum, gasping for breath. The air would be gone soon. Captain Nemo came in.

"Is the hole deep enough?" I gasped.

"I don't know," he said. "But we must try to break free anyway. It's our last chance!"

He ordered that the ballast tanks be filled with water. He hoped that they would make the submarine heavy enough to

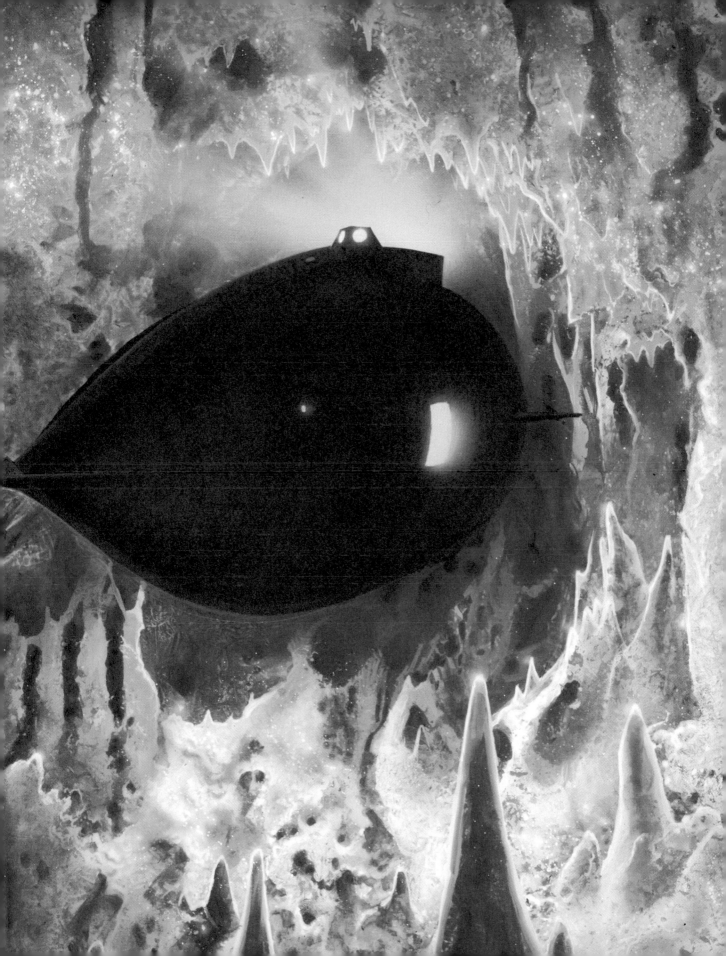

break through the ice. The wait seemed like an eternity.

Then we heard a loud cracking sound! The *Nautilus* lurched. I could feel it sinking! We had broken through! The order was given to surface. The submarine shot upward. As soon as we reached the surface, the hatch was thrown open and everyone rushed on deck. It was wonderful to breathe fresh air again!

I didn't ever want to get that close to dying again. But little did I know that a greater test of survival lay just ahead.

After a few days we reached the warmer waters of the Atlantic. Conseil was looking out the port window, when he suddenly asked: "Professor, how big do squids grow?"

"I have a friend," I said, "who once saw one that was more than fifteen feet long."

"Well, if this is not the one your friend saw, then it must be its brother!"

I rushed to the window. There I beheld a horrible sight. Not only was there one giant squid, there were seven! The *Nautilus* came to a sudden stop. I found the Captain working on the ship's instruments.

"One of the squids has gotten caught in the propeller," he said. "We will have to surface and get rid of them."

"Can we shoot them?"

"No. The electric bullets won't work on them," he said.

We came to the surface. As soon as the hatch opened, a long tentacle came slithering down the steps. Nemo chopped it off and headed on deck. It was a frightening sight on deck! There seemed to be hundreds of long, curling arms everywhere! Some of us struck at them with hatchets; others used harpoons.

Suddenly, I saw a squid grab up Captain Nemo. It lifted him high off his feet! In a moment he would be lost! He would be carried under the sea by the monster. Ned took aim and threw his harpoon at the squid. It was a perfect hit! The creature dropped the Captain and slid from the deck.

Soon, all the monsters were either dead or dying. The deck of the ship was slippery with their strange green blood. Before we went back down the ladder, Captain Nemo stopped Ned.

"You saved my life," he said to the harpooner. "Why?"

"I don't know," replied Ned.

From that day, Captain Nemo seemed very different. He kept to himself and rarely spoke. Something was wrong.

When we reached the North Atlantic, we were suddenly hit by a powerful storm. Instead of diving underwater to be safe, Nemo ordered that the ship remain on the surface. He even went on the deck to ride out the storm. Giant waves crashed over him. Lightning flashed all about him. I thought that he was trying to kill himself.

The next day I learned what was troubling the Captain. A ship had been following us!

"Our ship must have gotten back safely," I said. "They must have reported that it was not a monster attacking ships, but a submarine!"

Every day the ship got a little closer. Ned was curious as to what nation the ship belonged to. He got a telescope from the museum and took it on deck. But no sooner had he raised it to his eyes, than the Captain struck it from his hands. I had never seen him so angry.

"Get below!" he shouted.

"Are you going to attack that ship?" I asked.

"I'm going to sink it!"

"But whose ship is it?"

"You don't know? Good! Now get below!"

Soon we could hear the shots from the ship's cannons. The battle was under way.

"They're shooting at us!" said Conseil.

"What is the Captain going to do?" asked Ned.

"He's going to ram that ship!" I said. As I spoke I could feel

the *Nautilus* picking up speed. We were going faster and faster. Captain Nemo aimed his submarine at the ship like a missile.

It hit with a loud crash! The submarine was going so fast, it passed through the warship like a needle going through cloth!

The ship sank with everyone on board.

From that day on we did not see Captain Nemo. He kept to his room. The *Nautilus* seemed to wander the seas without a captain. Ned thought it was time to try an escape.

We chose one dark night. We would steal the little boat that was on deck of the *Nautilus*. Since the Captain never came out of his room, he wouldn't notice until it was too late.

It was dark inside the submarine as we crept from our rooms. A curious sound came to our ears. It was music. Nemo was in the museum playing his organ. Would he notice us?

We knew that we had to go through the salon in order to escape. My heart was beating fast. I opened the door of the salon as quietly as I could and we crept past. Slowly and quietly we sneaked to the ladder that led to the deck. Just then, I heard the last words I ever heard Captain Nemo speak.

"Almighty God!" he said. "Enough! Enough!"

We opened the hatch and went on deck. There seemed to be a fierce storm outside. Giant waves swirled around us. The *Nautilus* rolled like a bucking horse, and we could barely hold on.

"It's a whirlpool!" cried Ned. "Get to the boat before it sucks us all down!"

As we got in, the ship began whirling around faster and faster. Suddenly it threw the boat off the deck like a slingshot. I hit my head, and that's the last thing I remember.

I awoke in a fisherman's hut. Ned and Conseil were there. But what became of Nemo and the *Nautilus?* Did they disappear in the whirlpool? Did they escape? No one knows, but I pray they roam the oceans still.

Printing History 15 14 13 12 11 10 9 8 7 6 5 4 3 2 1

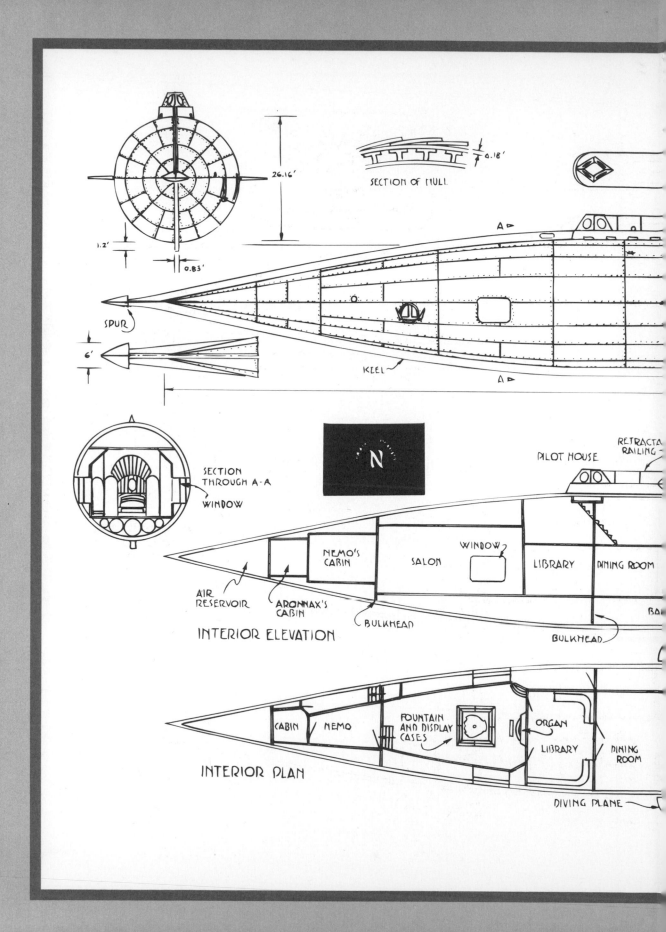

SECTION OF HULL

26.16'

1.2'

0.83'

SPUR

6'

KEEL

A ▷

A ▷

SECTION
THROUGH A-A

WINDOW

N

AIR
RESERVOIR

ARONNAX'S
CABIN

NEMO'S
CABIN

SALON

WINDOW

LIBRARY

DINING ROOM

BULKHEAD

BULKHEAD

PILOT HOUSE

RETRACTA
RAILING

BO

INTERIOR ELEVATION

CABIN

NEMO

FOUNTAIN
AND DISPLAY
CASES

ORGAN

LIBRARY

DINING
ROOM

INTERIOR PLAN

DIVING PLANE